For Mom, master wordsmith and resident
night creature; and for Dad, fountain of
kindness and teller of tales.

Rory Haltmaier is an award-winning artist, writer, and friend to all
creatures—especially those with wings. There's a good chance she
could tell you what kind of bird just flew past your window.

Visit her at roryhaltmaier.com
Instagram: @ror.creates

Tentacular Arts & Letters

Text, Illustration, and Design Copyright © 2021
by Rory Haltmaier

ISBN: 978-1-7374372-0-8

How Wonderfully Odd!

Written and Illustrated by
Rory Haltmaier

TENTACULAR
Arts & Letters

In the depths of a lush, green forest, creatures of the night buzzed and chirped, slithered and scurried. Some even flew, like Obie Owl and Bitsy Bat.

Every night while daytime creatures slept, Obie and Bitsy had adventures under a sky full of stars. They played hide-and-go-seek in the tall trees and hunted until their bellies were full. At sunrise, they returned home to sleep.

Obie and Bitsy were excited about their first sleepover, but Obie's older brother was a little uneasy about Bitsy Bat's way of sleeping.

"You know she sleeps upside down," he said. "Only daytime creatures are that odd."

"Is that really so odd?" Bitsy thought. Neither Bitsy nor Obie could say—they were nocturnal animals and had never even met a daytime creature.

"Let's stay up all day," Obie Owl said, "and see what daytime creatures are really like."

The pair tiptoed outside and flew off into the bright yellow morning.

Soon they were caught in a thick tangle of branches. A furry daytime creature named Squirrel popped over.

"Looking for a way through?"
Squirrel asked. "I can show you."

Obie and Bitsy nodded. They
followed Squirrel into the
maze of branches...

...but they quickly fell
behind. Bitsy Bat's
wing got tangled...

...and Obie Owl
almost took
a tumble!

Squirrel slowed down to check on the frazzled night creatures.

"Squirrels are natural acrobats," he said. "My big tail balances me as I jump from branch to branch so I never fall. Where's your bushy tail?"

"We can't climb or jump like you," Obie said, "but with our wings, we can soar far above the trees."

"And never get tangled," Bitsy added.

"How wonderfully odd," Squirrel said. "You can touch the clouds!"

Obie Owl and Bitsy Bat waved goodbye to Squirrel and flew off to a sparkling pond teeming with juicy bugs.

They weren't having much luck catching bugs in the bright sun. Suddenly, a slimy tongue shot past Bitsy Bat's head!

"You made me miss my lunch!" a wet creature with bulging eyes croaked.

"Sorry!" Bitsy said. "We haven't caught a single bug yet."

"Maybe I can help," offered the creature. "The name's Frog—and I'm the very best bug-catcher around."

The pair followed Frog onto the wobbly lily pads. They tried to copy Frog by sticking out their tiny tongues—but they still couldn't catch a thing.

Bitsy set her sights on a fly. She leaned…

…and stretched…

…and toppled into the water!

"I'm okay!" Bitsy spluttered. "Catching bugs like Frog is too hard."

"My tongue is long and sticky to pluck bugs out of the air," Frog said. "Where's your big tongue?"

"I use my big ears to catch bugs," Bitsy said. "I hear exactly where they are, even on the darkest nights. My mom calls it ech-o-lo-ca-tion. Then I gobble them up as I fly."

"And I use my big green eyes to spot prey from way up in the sky," Obie said. "Then I swoop down without a sound to snatch them up."

"How wonderfully odd," said Frog. "You're amazing hunters, too."

Rain began to pitter-patter on the pond.

"Uh oh. My feathers don't like getting wet. Time to go," Obie Owl said.

"I love being wet. Bye for now," Frog said, slipping under the water.

Flying in the wind and rain was hard, even for these expert fliers. A fierce gust almost swept the tiny night creatures away.

"We have to land!" Bitsy cried.

They crash-landed into
a patch of long grass,
shivering.

Obie Owl could have
sworn they were
being watched.

A moment later, an enormous
creature snarled behind them.

"Please don't gobble us up!"
Bitsy Bat shrieked.

"Don't be silly," the creature said. "My name is Badger. My burrow is right over there if you'd like to warm up."

Obie and Bitsy were very grateful.
Badger's burrow was warm and
dry but much too small.

"Let's make some more room,"
Badger said, beginning to dig.

Obie Owl's razor sharp
talons barely scratched
the dirt…

…and Bitsy Bat's curved
claws could only dig out
tiny clumps.

Badger dug with
such speed…

…that Obie and Bitsy
nearly disappeared under
a pile of dirt!

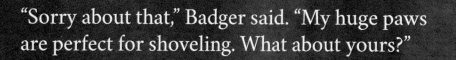

"Sorry about that," Badger said. "My huge paws are perfect for shoveling. What about yours?"

"Our claws are good for other things, like gripping tree branches," Obie Owl said.

"Or hanging upside down," Bitsy Bat added.

"How wonderfully odd," Badger said. "It's hard to imagine the world from high up in the trees."

The storm was over but Obie and Bitsy
were too tuckered out to notice—
it was way past their bedtime now.

Badger gently lifted them out and
sent them on their way home.

Obie's older brother was waiting for them back at the hollow. "Where have you been all day?" he squawked.

"We've been making friends with daytime creatures," Obie Owl said.

"You told us that daytime creatures were odd but they're not," Bitsy declared. "They're wonderfully odd! Just like me."

"You're absolutely right," a familiar voice croaked. Startled, the three turned around…

...to see Obie and Bitsy's daytime buddies in the doorway!

"We just wanted to make sure you made it home safe and sound," Frog said.

Obie and Bitsy beamed at the sight of
Frog, Squirrel, and Badger—but they just
couldn't keep their eyes open any longer.

They imagined playing with their
wonderfully odd new friends as they
drifted off to sleep.

Made in the USA
Middletown, DE
26 October 2022

13369117R00020